No Sniveling

a fluffy tail of Floppidy Loppidy

By Shirley and Lauren DeLong

No Sniveling

a fluffy tail of Floppidy Loppidy

Shirley & Lauren DeLong Illustrated by Designo Dream

ISBN: 978-0-9894180-0-3

Printed in China

Skunk Hollow Publishing
406 The Hill
Portsmouth, NH 03802
www.SkunkHollowPublishing.com

Hi, there. My name is Floppidy Loppidy,
and I'm pretty unique for a few reasons.
Any guesses? OK, silly pants, you got one of them,
but my long loppidy-floppidy ears are kind
of obvious, don't you think?
I'm also pretty special because I'm the one and only Easter
Rabbit's grandson. That's right.
How cool is that?

My friends don't always seem like friends
because they can be kind of mean
when they tease me.
They think my extra-extra-long floppy
ears are funny looking.
The Easter Rabbit always tells me
that my ears are special ears because
they allow me to hear for
miles and miles and miles.

My mom always tells me that my
ears are amazing long ears and that
they make me special in the
world. Mom says, "Floppidy Loppidy,
I have never met a bunny who can
hear everything so far and near—
even whispering!" Mom reminds me
that I am unique in all the world.
She always says, "Floppidy Loppidy,
remember that I love you… so
nooooooo sniveling!"

Guess what time of year it is. Yes, that's right!
Easter is coming—the busiest time of the year for bunnies.
More than anything, I'm totally going to help
my grandfather, the one and only Easter Rabbit, get ready.
No more crazy floppy-loppy ear accidents this year
where everyone laughs at me. Nope, no sir-ee, Bob.

I'm going to be an Easter hero. *No sniveling* here!

Aha! I know where I'm going to start.
Yup, that's right. I'm going to help
by painting the Easter eggs all the beautiful colors—
purple and pink, yellow and blue.
I can do that! Uh-oh! Oh, no!

Whoopsie whoops. As I was painting the eggs, I didn't know my extra-extra-long ears were dragging and dipping into all the pretty paint colors. Jeez Louise!

My bunny buddies are
going to tie my ears
into a bow again!
My amazing ears are a mess.
They're purple and pink,
yellow and blue!
Oh, well. It's OK.
"Floppidy Loppidy,"
Mom always says,
"accidents happen.
Nooooooo sniveling!"

I need to find a way to help without getting into messy wet paint. Oh, wait. I've got it! I'm going to help by filling the Easter baskets with all the wonderful green grass.
How could I possibly get messy with grass?

Here we go again! My amazing extra-extra-long ears
are dragging and flipping the grass everywhere,
even into the air, catching on my whiskers.
I'm starting to feel sneezy. I think I'm going to…ah, ahhhh,
ahhhhhhhhhhchooooooooo!
Uh-oh! Oh, no!

I hear you laughing, but the sneezles
and the wheezles are not funny!
Sure, flying grass might look
like super-cool green fireworks
exploding in the sky to you, but not to me.
My sneezing is sending all the wonderful
green grass everywhere—everywhere
except in the Easter baskets.
Flumpidy de dumpidy,
how am I going to explain this
mess to my grandfather,
the Easter Rabbit?

Oh, well. It's OK. "Floppidy Loppidy,"
Mom always says, "accidents happen.
Nooooooo sniveling!"

I know how I can be a mighty,
tidy hero! How difficult could it be?
I'll make sweet little yummy marshmallow chicks.
Every child loves yummy yellow chicks!
I'll just mix up the ingredients with a blender,
heat up the candy to make it extra icky sticky,
then pour the melted marshmallow
into the chick molds on cookie sheets.

Look at me! I am rocking this job!
I am doing such a neat and tidy job.
But wait…uh-oh! Oh, no!

You guessed it again! How did my extra-extra-long
ears trip me up this time?

And the icky-sticky-drippy warm marshmallow
slops and slides all over my soft, fluffy, bunny-fur tail.
What a mess! Oh, no! Don't tell me that
I'm going to land in a soupy-goopy pile
of yellow marshmallow! Oh, well. It's OK.
"Floppidy Loppidy," Mom always says,
"accidents happen.
Nooooooo sniveling!"

Harrrrumph! Why couldn't I be a reindeer instead?
I'd take a red nose over floppy ears any day.
Oh, wait. Did you hear that?
Help is needed to sort jellybeans.
That should be an easy-peasy, lemon-squeezy job.
The red jellybeans go in the red jar.
The yellow ones go in the yellow jar.
The green ones go in the green jar and so on.

Ooooops. I dropped one on the floor.
Not a worry here.
I'll just bend down and pick it up.
Uh-oh! Oh, no!

Hey, did you turn off the lights? I'm serious.
Who turned off the lights?
Ahhh, my extra-extra-long ears are covering my eyes.
How am I supposed to see with my ears over my eyes?

Smash, crash! Smash, crash! Smash, crash!
All the jars with all the jellybeans are all over the floor.
Oh, well. It's OK. "Floppidy Loppidy,"
Mom always says, "accidents happen.
Nooooooo sniveling!"

Oh, wait. What is that I hear? Hooray! Finally the Easter Rabbit has a wonderful idea— an important and really perfect job for me. The Easter Rabbit says, "Floppidy Loppidy, since your amazing extra-extra-long ears can hear so well, even whispering…

…would you check on all the precious
little children around the world waiting
for Easter and listen for sweetness or sniveling?
The Easter Rabbit asked Floppidy Loppidy
to create a sniveling report each day.
The children who do not snivel and are cheerful
and kind will find an extra-extra-sweet treat in their
basket on Easter morning."

So every day I use my satellite-dish-like ears
to listen for sniveling, and then at night
I report back and give my sniveling
report to the Easter Rabbit.

Ahhh, all done.
Another day passes without any accidents.
I just listen to all the little children.
This is the best! Now I can snuggle to
sleep with all of my bunny buddies.
They love how I wrap my extra-extra-wonderful
long ears around them,
warming, protecting, and cuddling them close.
I whisper what my mom always whispers to me,
"Sweet dreams. *No sniveling!*"

Hippity hoppity!
Easter's on its way!

As I fall asleep, I
smile, and all my
bunny buddies call
me a hero! No more
extra-long ear teasing
for me!

22